W9-DGV-946

617107
$14.95
Rainbow

NASCAR Champions

DALE JARRETT

Lincoln James

New York

Published in 2007 by The Rosen Publishing Group, Inc.
29 East 21st Street, New York, NY 10010

Book Design: Michael J. Flynn

Photo Credits: Cover (Jarrett) © Jon Ferry/Allsport; cover (background) © Robert Laberge/Allsport; pp. 5, 7 © Bill Hall/Allsport; p. 9 © Andy Lyons/Getty Images; pp. 11, 21 © Craig Jones/Allsport; p. 13 © Allen Steele/Allsport; pp. 15, 17 © David Taylor/Getty Images; p. 19 © Brian Bahr/ Getty Images.

Library of Congress Cataloging-in-Publication Data

James, Lincoln.
  Dale Jarrett / Lincoln James.
     p. cm. — (NASCAR champions)
  Includes index.
  ISBN-13: 978-1-4042-3459-4
  ISBN-10: 1-4042-3459-4 (lib. bdg.)
 1. Jarrett, Dale, 1956—Juvenile literature. 2. Automobile racing drivers—United States—Biography—Juvenile literature. I. Title. II. Series.
GV1032.J37J26 2007
796.72092-dc22
 (B)
                                  2006014310

Manufactured in the United States of America

"NASCAR" is a registered trademark of the National Association for Stock Car Auto Racing, Inc.

Contents

Dale Jarrett began racing cars in 1977. He was 20 years old.

4

5

Dale's father Ned was also
a race car driver. He won two
NASCAR championships.

6

Dale has four children. This is his son Zachary.

9

Dale's son Jason is also a race car driver.

11

Dale's first NASCAR race was in 1982. He won his first NASCAR race in 1991.

13

Dale won the Daytona 500 three times. The Daytona 500 is one of the biggest races each year.

15

In 1999, Dale won the NASCAR championship. This meant he won 2 million dollars!

NASCAR
Winston Cup Champion

PAY TO THE ORDER OF _Dale Jarrett_   2,000,000.00

Two million & 00/100 _____ DOLLARS

MEMO _1999 Championship_   FROM Winston
R.J. Reynolds Tobacco Company

17

Dale is on the list of NASCAR's 50 Greatest Drivers. So is his father Ned!

18

19

Dale raises money to help people. He likes to help children.

EXIDE NASCAR
SELECT BATTERIES 400

21

Glossary

championship (CHAM-pea-uhn-ship)
A contest held to see who is the best
in a sport.

Daytona 500 (day-TOH-nuh FYV
HUN-druhd) The famous first NASCAR
race every year. It is held in Daytona
Beach, Florida.

raise (RAYZ) To gather something
together, such as money.

Books and Web Sites

Books

Buckley, James. *NASCAR*. New York: DK Children, 2005.

Gigliotti, Jim. *Dale Jarrett: It Was Worth the Wait.* Chanhassen, MN: Child's World, 2002.

Web Sites

Due to the changing nature of Internet links, PowerKids Press has developed an online list of Web sites related to the subject of this book. This site is updated regularly. Please use this link to access the list:

http://www.powerkidslinks.com/NASCAR/jarrett/

Index